The Adventu... ...f Zelda:
The Second Saga

The Adventures of Zelda:
The Second Saga

Kristen Otte

The Adventures of Zelda: The Second Saga

First Print Edition: 2014

Editor: Candace Johnson
Cover Design: Michael McFarland

ISBN: 1494424398
ISBN-13: 978-1494424398

This book is dedicated to those who enjoyed the first collection of Zelda adventures and encouraged me to keep writing about a silly, wrinkly pug.

Table of Contents

Chapter 1
The Empty Room

I can't believe a year has passed since my family adopted me. The past year was filled with every sort of adventure. I conquered Vacuum, the leaf pile, and the skate park. I became friends with Tucker, Whitney, and Squeaks; I survived attacks from Jack Jack, the Snowman, and Gannondorf. Although the excitement has waned in the past few weeks, I know another adventure will cross my path soon.

My new adventure arrived a week ago with the appearance of boxes. Boxes usually live in the basement, but for the past week, they have multiplied into every room of the house. I have no idea what is inside the boxes. Most of them are closed, and I am too short to see in them, even when standing on my hind legs. The worst part is they are taking up most of the floor. My pug sprints are contained to a small circle around the coffee table in the living room. Pug sprints are not supposed to be contained to small spaces.

After a week of the boxes piling up, they begin to disappear almost as quickly and quietly as they appeared. Nate and Hannah have been carrying the boxes to the car. Hannah and Nate return later, but not the boxes.

Where are the boxes going? I hope I don't end up in one of them!

The boxes are a mystery, and I know I am the right pug to solve it. With only a few boxes remaining in the living room, I have a limited amount of time. I need a quick, decisive plan. One of the remaining boxes is open and next to the couch. I hop onto the couch and look inside the box. I don't see anything sharp or spiky, so I back up, get a running start, and jump into the box. I land on a hard, slippery surface and slide into the other side. I gather myself and use my paw to shut one flap of the box. I lie underneath it to conceal myself.

I start to fall asleep in the box when I hear Nate coming my way. My heart starts beating faster as I think about where Nate might take the box and me. My nerves get the best of me, and the hiccups start.

Nate is going to find my hiding spot!

But Nate never picks up my box. I hear him turn around and walk in the opposite direction. I breathe a sigh of relief, my heartbeat slows, and my hiccups dissipate. When I hear footsteps a second time, I am as silent and motionless as a stone. Nate picks up the box. But the box is crooked. I slide in the opposite direction, crashing into the other side.

"Zelda, what are you doing in here?" he asks. I bark, trying to signal my intention to go with him. He puts the box down, lifts me up, and puts me on the ground.

"It's not time for you to go yet," he says. "But soon, Z. Hang in there." Nate lifts the box and carries it outside. I am so frustrated and disappointed that I lie right where Nate put me. I close my eyes and fall asleep.

I wake up to movement and voices.

"We need to lock Zelda up so she doesn't get trampled," Hannah says.

"She's not going to like that," Ben says.

"I know, but it needs to happen. Why don't you put her in the crate for the next few hours?" Hannah replies. Before I realize what is happening, Ben is carrying me. He puts me in the crate in the corner of the room. I bark a few times, but I know it's pointless; I heard Hannah's words.

I watch the action from inside the crate. It's chaos. Everything is in motion—the couch, chairs, people, and boxes. I have never seen anything like it. I can't see where anything is going, but I assume it is out the door.

I lose track of time, entranced by the scene in front of me. When Ben finally lets me out of the crate, the living room has transformed. There is nothing left in it except my crate, food bowl, and water dish. I don't even have any toys.

What is going on?

"Zelda, we will be back for you in a few hours," Ben says. He walks over and pets me before leaving out the front door. I walk to the window and see Ben walk into a big white and orange truck. I explore the other rooms of the house and find the same scene. Every room is empty—no beds, chairs, or bookcases. I return to the living room and look out the window, hoping Lucy and Ben will be outside waiting for me. They aren't.

I walk toward my crate to lie down, and then I notice the closet door is open a crack. I paw the door completely open; Vacuum is staring back at me. I immediately bark twice at her.

I am not scared of Vacuum since I tore her arm off, but we are not on good terms. I don't trust her. I constantly remind her that I am the head of the family.

Why would they leave me alone with Vacuum?

I walk over to my crate and lie down. I am completely stumped; I don't know what to do or what is happening. I go back over the conversation from earlier. Ben said they would be back for me. He wouldn't lie, and my family wouldn't leave me behind. I start to close my eyes, but I see Vacuum out of the corner of my eye.

What about Vacuum?

As much as I don't like Vacuum, I know they can't leave her behind, either. It wouldn't be right. She's been with the family almost as long as I have. She is a bit of a bully. On the other hand, she adds mystery and adventure to my life.

I know what I need to do.

I get up and walk over to Vacuum. I bark once to let her know I'm on her side. Then I grab one of her arms and start pulling her toward my crate, but she topples over onto the ground.

Whoops.

I grab her arm again and start pulling. She's heavier than I remember, but I have enough strength. After an exhausting few minutes, Vacuum is next to my crate. I tell her to get up, but she doesn't listen, and after a few minutes of trying, I give up. There is no way I can get her standing again.

I walk into my crate and lie down. It was exhausting work, but hopefully my family will understand.

I wake up to the front door opening.

"Zelda, it's time to go to your new home," Hannah says. I dart to her and greet her with a lick to the face to show my appreciation for her return. "It's good to see you, too."

"What happened here?" she asks, walking to Vacuum. "Did you get mad at the vacuum again?" she says with a laugh. "Okay, let's get you loaded up."

Hannah takes my crate, food bowl, and water dish to her car. She returns inside and grabs my leash. I run over to Vacuum and bark.

"It's time to go," Hannah says, coming toward me with the leash. I dart away, and she follows me. I sprint back to Vacuum and grab her arm, pulling her toward the door.

"No, Zelda, leave it," Hannah says. I can't mess up my chance to leave with Hannah, so I obey against my instincts. I slowly walk to the door. Hannah leashes me, and we go for a ride, leaving Vacuum behind.

Should I have done more?

The ride is surprisingly short. We pull into the driveway of an unfamiliar house. The big truck is there, along with Nate's black car. I jump out of the car, and Hannah leads me up the front steps.

"Hi, Z Bug," Lucy says as I enter the house. She bends over and gives me a pet on my forehead wrinkles. I sneeze in her face; for some reason, petting my forehead always makes me sneeze.

"C'mon, I will show you our new house." Lucy takes the leash from Hannah.

Lucy leads me through the house—the living room, dining room, kitchen, and bedrooms. This house has two stairways! One stairway goes down; the other goes up. I recognize much of the stuff in the house—my couch and chair, the beds, and the boxes. The house is bigger than the last—so much more room for pug sprints. I can't wait to try it out when the boxes disappear.

After our tour, Lucy takes me back to the living room. Hannah and Nate are sitting together on the couch, and Ben's in the chair. I jump into Nate's lap.

"Welcome to your new home, Zelda," Nate says. Mystery solved. The boxes and I are in a new home. I reach up and lick Nate's face.

Chapter 2
The Slippery Floor

After a few days at the new house, the boxes disappear from the floor and provide me with room to roam and sprint and play. I grab my owl and take it to Ben, who is sitting on the couch in the living room. He throws the owl into the dining room. I jump off the couch for the owl. When I land, I lose my footing and slide. I see the owl a few sprints away and try to run for it. But I can't gain any traction on the floor. I flail on the slippery floor until I finally make it to the owl. I grab it with my mouth and trot to Ben.

On the next throw, I jump more carefully off the couch and land successfully. As I gain speed, I lose control again. I slide into the owl first and the dining room table second. I hear Ben and Nate laughing in the background. I grab the owl and bring it to Lucy. She isn't laughing. She throws the owl in the opposite direction, and it lands in front of the closet. I sprint the first few paces and then attempt to slow down, grab the owl, and turn around. My plan fails. Instead of turning around, I sail into the closet, grabbing the owl along the way. I crash into the wall in the back of the closet. I turn to my right. Vacuum is next to me.

How did Vacuum get to this new house? I thought she was left behind. Do they know she is here? Maybe she isn't supposed to be here!

I drop the owl and start barking. I need to tell Hannah and Nate that Vacuum is here.

"What is it, Zelda?" Nate says. Lucy walks over to me.

"It's the vacuum, Daddy," she says.

"Not again," Nate says. "Zelda, leave it."

Oh well.

I pick up the owl and run for the open spot on the couch between Ben and Nate. As I jump for the couch, I lose my footing again. I'm in trouble. I don't have enough height to land on the couch, but I'm in motion, unable to stop.

Crash.

My right side smashes into the side of the couch. Luckily, when I lose my traction, I also tilt to the right so I don't hit the couch headfirst. I recover quickly and make the jump on the couch. But after taking the hit, I don't feel well. I lie down next to Ben and close my eyes.

I wake up later to an empty couch and a dry tongue. I don't hear any movement; the family must have left. I slowly jump off the couch and head for the water bowl. I manage to jump successfully onto the slippery floor, but my right side is throbbing. As I stick my head in the water bowl, I realize what I have to do. I need to master the slippery floor. I can't keep sliding and missing jumps all over the place. First, it's painful. And second, what happens if I slide into Vacuum next time? I don't want to experience her reaction.

Since the family is away, I start my training immediately. My right side is sore, but I'm a resilient pug. The first step is to determine how fast I can run on the floor without slipping. I walk across the floor, and each time I return to the couch, I go a little faster. When I hit a slow run, I brace for impact with the couch. Surprisingly, I can run at a jog without slipping.

But any run faster than a jog is trouble. I don't think I will ever pug sprint on this floor.

I train my body at a jogging speed, jogging around the coffee table, dining room, and kitchen. I have to use all my pug concentration to jog because my instincts tell me sprinting is way more fun. The training lasts five jogs around the house before I am ready for a nap. I yawn and lie down.

When my family returns, I am ready for a romp with the owl. I greet Ben and Lucy by jumping and licking their faces. I grab the owl, squeak it three times, and bring it to Lucy. She and I play tug-of-war for a few minutes until I allow her to take the owl. She immediately throws it across the room. I jog to the owl, grab it, and bring it back without a single slip or mess up. Lucy takes the owl again and throws it the opposite direction. I fetch it again. Lucy tries to grab the owl from my mouth, but I play keep-away. She chases me around the coffee table and catches up to me quickly. She grabs the owl and throws it again; this time it lands in the dining room. I run toward the owl, but Ben appears out of nowhere, snatches the owl, and runs toward me. I freeze for a second before jogging across the room. Ben chases after me, and I keep running. I feel my excitement rising, and, before I know it, the sprinting has started. I jump from the couch to the chair and then back to the floor. I dash across the floor without hesitation. Somehow I make it into the dining room, but when I try to turn, I slide into a chair. I don't care; I keep running through every room, sliding along the way.

When the haze settles, I find myself on the couch resting next to Lucy. I sneeze and lick her face a few times. As I settle down from my pug-sprint high, I realize there is no way I will ever stop pug sprinting. It's too much fun, even with the risk of hurting myself and crashing into furniture or Vacuum. I need to find a different method to conquer the slippery floor.

The next day, my family leaves for school and work. I am home alone again, and every fiber of me wants to keep sleeping. However, I have my own work to do. I need to learn how to run on this floor.

I start training. When I begin to slide, I try to keep running. But it's not working. I have no control over my paws. I get another running start and accidentally begin sliding toward the coffee table. I stop moving my legs in the hope that I will slow down and miss it. I don't slow down enough and so I crash into the table, but as I hit the table, I realize I am sliding straight.

I've got it!

I can harness the sliding to my advantage. I get up again and try sliding in the middle of the room. When my paws start slipping, I freeze and slide forward until I slow enough to start running again.

It works!

I try again and slide under the dining room table and then run on the other side. It's perfect; sliding is so much fun! I can't wait to try it out with my family.

When the family walks into the house, I immediately bring a ball to Hannah.

"Not yet, Zelda," Hannah says.

Nate walks in behind the family carrying something big and blue. He sets it down and I investigate, but I smell nothing good. Nate moves the coffee table to one side of the room and fumbles with the big blue thing. Finally, he sets it down on the floor, and it grows as he walks across the room. It's amazing. I run on it and follow until I reach its edge.

What is it?

It now covers up a large portion of the floor; it is much softer than the floor and feels like the floor of our old house. I jog from one side to the other without a slip. I bring the ball back to Hannah. This time, she obliges and throws the ball across the room. I sprint across the blue thing. It moves as I move. The sensation is weird.

"Here, Zelda, let me put the coffee table back. Then the rug won't move," Hannah says, moving the coffee table to the center of the blue thing.

Wait, what won't move? The floor?

I grab the ball again and bring it back to Hannah. The ball sails into the dining room. I run across the blue thing, and nothing happens this time. I slide into the ball and sprint back.

"Do you like the rug?" Hannah asks.

The rug? I guess that's the blue thing.

I grab the ball one more time and bring it to Hannah. She throws it again, and I run my fastest across the rug. I stop flailing when I hit the floor. As my slide slows, I start running again for the ball. I take it and run back. I have mastered the floor. The new house isn't anything this pug can't handle.

Chapter 3
The Fenced Backyard

"Time to go outside Zelda," Nate yells. I run for the front door, ready for a walk or an adventure outside.

"Zelda, this way, come here," Nate says. I wander to Nate's voice and find him standing in front of a wide-open back door. I stand, confused. First, Nate doesn't have a leash. Second, for the first week at the new home, the family took me out in the front yard. I thought it was odd because there is a door straight out to the backyard. I even tried to lead Nate and Ben to the back, but they never gave in to my request.

"Zelda, let's go out," Nate says again and walks out the door. I don't hesitate this time. If he isn't going to leash me, I am running for it. I sprint out the door into the yard.

I run straight as far as I can go. I stop inches before I hit a piece of wood sticking up out of the grass. I stop and look around. The wood surrounds the yard on all sides. The backyard is fenced, like Tucker and Whitney's yard. But this yard is different. At Tucker and Whitney's, I can't see through the fence except for a few tiny cracks here and there. This fence has gaps everywhere that allow me to see into our neighbors' yards.

I run from corner to corner, inspecting the fence, investigating for good smells, and checking out our neighbors' yards. Along the back fence line are a few large trees. We have neighbors on two sides and in the back. The back fence is laced with great smells. From what I can deduce from my sniffer, the smells are squirrel, cat, and dog. I hope I am right!

"C'mon, Zelda, time to go inside," I hear Nate yell from the door. I jog back to the house and in the door.

"Do you like the fenced backyard?" he asks. I stand on my hind legs and lick his fingers. "I thought you might," Nate mumbles. He walks over to the counter and hands me a treat. Nate is right. I love the backyard and can't wait to go outside again.

The next day, I have my second chance to explore the backyard. This time, Ben and Lucy come out with me. They throw a ball, and I play keep-away with them until I get bored. I start sniffing again, eager to figure out exactly what the squirrels are up to in this yard. I find a strong scent, and it leads me into some bushes and plants next to a tree along the back fence line. The scent is definitely squirrel, and it is heading up the tree. I look up for squirrel signs or markings, and suddenly my nose is overwhelmed by a powerful dog smell.

The smell starts me on a sneezing attack. When I recover from my fit, I am looking into the nose of an eight-pugs' worth dog. He is brown like me with a streak of white on his belly; he is sticking his long nose through the fence slots.

A dog! Next door! I want to play with him!

I start scratching at the fence, trying to find a weak spot. If I can make a pug-sized hole or gap, we could play together every day! I run from one side of the fence to the other while he lies down in the grass. He watches me with a smirk.

"Zelda, leave it," Nate says firmly.

I keep running back and forth, looking for a hole. Nate starts chasing me; I'm now trying to dodge him and find a way to meet the dog. Nate catches up to me and picks me up before I have a chance to meet the dog. I squirm, but he has a firm hold on me.

"Settle down, Zelda. And leave Louie alone. He's too big to play with anyway," Nate says.

He's wrong. I can stand my ground with any dog, no matter how big.

He carries me into the house, and I know my next adventure—finding a way through the fence.

On my next visit to the backyard, Hannah lets me out and leaves me alone. All is quiet in the yard, so I investigate the fence again. I start in the middle by the tree and look for a gap big enough to squeeze through to the other yard. My head is so small that I can fit it through every slot, but my broad, bulldog-like shoulders are too wide.

I circle to the corner and see a gap wider than any of the other gaps between a few plants. I get closer and stick my head through and begin to shimmy the rest of my body. I suck in my belly and take a few more steps before I realize I am in. *I made it through the fence!* I look around and find myself behind a building in the middle of weeds, grass, and plants. As I sneeze, I look through the fence and realize I've made a mistake. This isn't the yard I want to explore. This yard is next to the dog's yard.

"Zelda," Hannah calls. I sneak back through the fence to our yard and run to her. I can't let Hannah know how I got out or she will never let me out here again. For some reason, my family thinks if they let me loose, I won't come back. It's a silly idea, and simply not true. I know how good I have it at home, but pugs need freedom and adventure.

Later on that evening, Nate opens the back door, and I can smell my friend right away. I look and see him hanging out in his yard with a green ball in his mouth. About halfway to the fence line, I stop and turn around. If I run to the fence again, Nate is going to make me come inside. It takes all my pug focus to stop and wander back toward the house, casually sniffing as I go. I see Nate watching me from the door, so I plop down in the grass. Nate walks away. I give him a couple seconds to return, but he doesn't.

I probably don't have much time, so I bolt to the corner, get skinny, and squeeze through the fence. Once in the other yard, I look around and get my bearings. I am next to a shed. I see no way to the other yard from this corner, so I walk to the front of the shed. The fence on this side is completely closed up like Tucker and Whitney's house. This isn't going to work. I sit for a moment, pug stumped.

"Hey cutie," I hear from afar. I see a woman with white hair approaching me from the house.

Uh oh.

I sprint around the shed to the corner and run through one of the slots. I get my shoulders through, but the slot is tight around my stomach.

Did I run through the wrong one?

I take a deep breath, try again, and somehow, my pug butt fits through the slot.

"Zelda, what are you doing?" Nate says to me. I look up and see Nate staring at me. "Let's go inside." I follow him, anticipating a scolding, but he doesn't say a word. He must not have seen me slip through the fence.

The next day I am astounded when Hannah lets me out again. My dog friend isn't out again, but I go to examine my secret escape place. Across the bottom of the fence is a new piece of wood covering the gap. Nate did see me sneak back into the yard. My escape is gone.

I wander around the yard, looking for an alternate spot to sneak out. I see a few more boards on the fence, and I realize my search is a lost cause. I am stuck in the backyard. I lie down in the middle of it in the sunshine. I look around and realize how much space I do have to run in the yard. I hear a rustle in the trees above me. I look up and see two squirrels chasing each other from branch to branch high above. I remember the fun I had with Squeaks, and I smile. I will have a good time in this yard.

Chapter 4
The New Neighborhood

I love the new house. I like sleeping in Hannah and Nate's bed during the day. The sunlight shines through the window, warming me as I lie on the bed. I love running up and down the stairs after Lucy and Ben. The fenced backyard is fantastic. I can stay outside for hours watching the squirrels and birds. But I do have one problem with the move—the neighborhood.

At the old house, the daily walks took us past a school and through a park. I was able to play in the skate park and investigate the millions of canine smells in the park. Even the streets were great. They were lined with towering, squirrel-filled trees, and the houses were packed with barking dogs.

The new neighborhood is much different. The houses are spaced far apart. I have no park to explore, and the trees are small and scarce. I haven't even seen a squirrel yet! I don't like the neighborhood one bit.

Even though I don't like it, I take my walks every day. I can't turn down the chance to explore and get my legs moving. After a few weeks of boring walks, I am determined to find something fun about the neighborhood.

Today, I decide to lead Ben and Nate on a different path. Usually we walk on the same two streets in a circle. Instead of making the loop, I lead Ben and Nate straight. I see more of the same—quiet houses with a small tree or two in the yard. As we walk, I begin to hear a faint whirring sound. At the next intersection, I turn left in the direction of the sound.

The whirring sound becomes louder and louder with every step. Soon, the whirring becomes a roar. The houses disappear into a sea of pavement and sidewalk. The road buzzes with a stream of cars and trucks. I slow our pace as we near the busy street. I stop and try to turn Ben and Nate around, but they won't let me. We turn left and follow the sidewalk along the busy street.

In the place of houses are very large buildings and sidewalk. The only grass in sight is a small strip separating the sidewalk from the street. With the cars whizzing by, I stay on the sidewalk and keep up a good pace in the hope that we can get back in a neighborhood soon. My nose is overwhelmed with unfamiliar scents as we walk. I don't recognize any of the odors; surely they can't be from dogs or even cats. I walk faster. I need to get off this street.

We keep walking for what seems like an eternity in the concrete jungle. Finally, we turn left again. The traffic slows a bit, and I see familiar houses up ahead. I breathe a sigh of relief and slow my pace. We turn down our street and finish up the walk. Ben, Nate, and I head inside. Hannah is waiting for us.

"That was a long walk," she says.

"It was," Nate says. He takes off my harness. Ben walks into the kitchen.

"Where did you go?" Hannah asks.

"We walked a loop to Harwich, Center Street, and Eastbrook Avenue," Nate says. Hannah's eyes widened.

"Wow, you walked Zelda on Center Street. That seems like a bad idea," she says.

"It was fine. And it probably won't happen again. Z was eager to get off Center Street," Nate says.

"Oh, good."

That's for sure. I'm not going that way again.

I find my owl and bring it to Ben. We play fetch, but my mind is preoccupied. I can't get the neighborhood off my brain. I need to find something fun for my walks. I can't help it. I'm a stubborn yet adventurous pug. Tomorrow we will explore a different street. There has to be something exciting here.

The next day I lead Hannah in the opposite direction from the busy street. When we turn right, I feel good. The road curves, the houses are even more spaced out, and the number of trees increases. I scurry from tree to tree, sniffing for signs of adventure. Without a trace of squirrel, we keep walking.

On the next intersection, I try to lead Hannah left again.

"Zelda, I'm not sure we should go that way," she says. "We will be walking for a long time." I ignore her pleadings and keep lunging left.

"Okay. Okay. We will go this way for a little bit, but then we need to turn around," she says. The houses are almost nonexistent at this point. And in the distance I see something dark covering the ground. As we approach, I realize it's water.

A pond!

I sprint for the pond, but Hannah yanks me back. The excitement and the jerk from Hannah trigger my short breathing. I start goose honking. When I regain control of myself, I calmly walk toward the pond, pretending that nothing happened.

An odor in the air grows as we near the pond. It's a new smell that isn't very pleasant. I walk off the sidewalk toward the pond to investigate. I quickly notice the culprit—droppings from animals, and they are everywhere. The smell tells me the droppings originate from an animal that isn't a dog or a cat.

We keep walking toward the water. I look for signs of life in and around the pond. Across the pond is a new creature that reminds me of a big duck. It has a long, black neck and a stripe of white by its mouth. The feathers are a gray color. I bark at it from across the pond, and its wings spread. I try to lead Hannah around the pond.

"C'mon Zelda, you don't want to meet a goose," she says, pulling me in the opposite direction.

But I do!

I lie down in the grass. I am not moving another inch. Hannah groans. She walks toward the goose on the other side of the pond. I jump up and lead the way.

When we are one pug sprint away from the goose, she leads me farther away from the pond. I guess she doesn't want to get too close, but I don't understand why. I am not going to hurt the goose. We walk by, and I hear a noise coming from it.

Hiiissssss.

Without thinking, I bark back.

"Zelda, no! Quiet!" Hannah shouts to me. I look toward the goose. It hasn't moved. It is sitting along the edge of a pond in a bed of twigs and grass. The goose doesn't want anything to do with us. That's a bit of a bummer, but maybe I can find something else to play with by the pond. Hannah leads me around the pond to circle back to the sidewalk. We walk slowly as I investigate every interesting smell.

We are almost back at the sidewalk when Hannah gasps.

"Uh oh," she mutters. "Let's go, Z." She pulls me forward.

Hiiissssss.

I look behind me. A goose is a few steps away and flapping its wings at us. The other goose is unmoving next to the pond. I am confused.

What is wrong? What did we do?

Before I can figure it out, the goose charges toward us. Hannah and I run to the sidewalk. She is running as fast as I am; I don't think she has ever kept up with me. I feel a rush of wings fly over us. Hannah stops. We both turn and look. The angry goose is out of sight. The other is sitting by the pond.

"That was a close one," Hannah whispers. "C'mon, Zelda, let's go home." I don't object this time. We trot at a steady pace to the sidewalk and back on the road home. When we arrive, the rest of the family is in the living room.

"How was your walk?" Nate asks.

"Terrifying," Hannah says, taking off my harness. I find a spot in Lucy's lap. She massages my body as I listen.

"What did Zelda do?" Nate says.

"It wasn't Zelda this time. We were at the pond on Greenview when we were chased by a goose." Nate and Ben both started laughing.

"No way," Ben says.

"Yes, way," Hannah says, defending herself. "One goose was sitting in her nest, most likely on her eggs, and I guess we got too close. Before we knew it, another goose flew at us, hissing and flapping its wings."

"So what did you do?" Nate asks.

"We ran!" Hannah says, laughing. "I guess it does sound a bit ridiculous."

"I don't believe it," Ben says.

"Oh, believe it. I couldn't make that story up," she replies.

"Well, I'm glad everyone is okay," Nate says. He walks over to Hannah and gives her a kiss.

"Ewww," Ben says. Hannah and Nate smile.

I join in the fun and lick Lucy's face. She smiles and laughs. Both of my attempts at adventures in the new neighborhood have been disasters. Maybe I need to suck it up and adapt to the new normal route. It's not the park or the streets lined with squirrel-filled trees, but it is good enough. I get to walk twice a day with my family. Most pugs dream of a life with two daily walks. I think I will be okay.

Chapter 5
Zelda and the Pillow Thief

I love bedtime. Every night, I curl up under the covers with Lucy, and she pets me until we fall asleep. I wake up the next morning refreshed and ready for another day of adventure.

Since we moved in to the new home, I am having trouble sleeping. After I crawl under the blankets with Lucy I try to fall asleep, but I can't. It's too hot, and the air is stuffy. I feel like I am going to pant the night away. So, I move out from under the blankets and sleep next to her. I end up waking up every few hours; she tosses and turns all night.

I tried sleeping in the living room on the couch or in my dog bed, but I don't like sleeping alone, and it's a bit chilly in the living room at night. I tried Hannah and Nate's bed, but they kicked me out. Ben is worse than Lucy at tossing and turning, so I didn't even last in his bed for one whole night.

I am back at square one, trying to get some rest with Lucy. I need to get my pug beauty sleep so I have enough energy to chase squirrels, run through leaf piles, and do well at school.

Tonight, I find a great spot next to Lucy under the covers at her feet. I don't feel hot like normal, so I close my eyes. I jerk awake from a kick to the back from Lucy. Aggravated, I crawl and lie next to her stomach, out of harm's way. But she feels like a hot, sunny walk, so I keep crawling until my head is out of the blankets and resting next to Lucy's head on the pillow. My head sinks into it; I breathe in the fresh air and relax.

I wake up a few hours later, overheated again. Lucy has rolled away from me, so I scoot onto the pillow and spread out. My whole body sinks into it. It feels incredible; the pillow is by far the best bed in the house. I fall asleep instantly and sleep through the night. I don't even wake up when Lucy leaves. How have I not slept here before?

The following night I have no hesitation. I jump on the bed and go straight for the pillow. But Lucy's head is in the middle of the pillow.

Pillow thief! I have to get it back.

I lie next to her with my head on the pillow, hoping she will move away from me and relinquish the pillow. I am lying there waiting when a big yawn comes over me. The next thing I remember is light peeking through the curtain the next morning. I open my eyes, and Lucy is right next to my head on the pillow, eyes closed and fast asleep. My plan failed.

The next night, I jump into Lucy's bed before her, and I sprawl out on the pillow. I fall asleep instantly. I awake to a conversation.

"Look, Mom, Zelda stole my pillow," Lucy says.

"She sure did," Hannah replies with a smile. "But you can move her out of the way. She's only a pug."

Only a pug?

But at that moment, Hannah grabs me and moves me off the pillow. I squirm and fight it, but it's too late. Lucy has claimed her spot. I'm stuck sleeping next to her again. I crawl my way to my spot, head to head with Lucy on my pillow, when I devise the perfect plan to get my pillow back.

I stay awake and wait for Lucy's eyes to close and her breathing to become regular. In a few minutes, she is asleep. I crawl up the pillow, step across her head, and lie down with my body sprawled across the pillow and her head.

Sure enough, in a few minutes, Lucy wakes up confused and rolls out from under me to the other side of the bed. I am so excited that I almost get up and lick her face when I remember she might take that opportunity to steal the pillow again. I lie down on it with my front paws touching one end and my back paws at the other end. And soon enough, I am dreaming about a world with endless peanut butter, steak, and a friend to play with everyday.

Chapter 6
A Pug Scary Story

On this warm autumn evening, my family is gone. I am keeping watch over the house. The house is completely dark. Hannah and Nate didn't leave the lamp lit in the living room. I walk upstairs to Hannah and Nate's bedroom looking for any traces of light. Luckily the curtains are open, providing a few streaks of light that bounce off the wall and create dancing shadows. I sit on the bed, staring out the window, looking for any signs of life. The nearly empty tree branches are swaying with the breeze, but not a soul is on the street.

The combination of the stillness and darkness makes me sleepy. I lie down on the bed. And before I know it, I drift to sleep.

Crackle, Crash!

I lift my head, listen, and wait. I hear a rustling noise from downstairs. I jump off the bed and creep down the stairs. The noise stops when I reach the bottom of the steps. I wait for a minute. I turn to go upstairs when I hear it again.

Crackle, Crash!

It sounds like the noise is coming from Vacuum's closet. I sidestep to the closet and peer inside. The darkness is overwhelming. I use my nose to guide me. I smell nothing unusual except Vacuum's terrible odor. My eyes adjust, and I see her resting in the corner under the coats. The remainder of the closet is empty.

Strange.

I back out of the closet slowly, waiting for any movement or noise. I wait for a few minutes and head back to my bed upstairs. Maybe my ears deceived me. In another few minutes, I am on the verge of a fabulous nap.

Crash. Boom.

The noise is louder and more distinct. It is definitely inside the house. Once again, I walk downstairs and investigate. I check over and under the couch. I check the dining room. I check every nook in the kitchen, but I see nothing unusual. I tiptoe to the living room and check Vacuum's closet again.

Wasn't Vacuum on the other side of the closet last time?

I swear she was under the coats earlier. But this time, she is standing at the entrance. I bark and wait for a response, but as usual she stays silent. Vacuum only responds on her terms.

Instead of going back to the bedroom, I find a comfortable spot on the couch. I will be ready to spot any trouble if I stay down here. I sit and wait. As I wait, I have trouble keeping my eyes open. My head falls into my paws, and I drift into dreamland.

RRRRROARRRR.

What is that?

I spring to my feet and jump off the couch in the direction of the closet. I don't waste any time; I slide straight into Vacuum at the entrance of the closet.

RRRRROARRRR.

Vacuum thunders toward me with her front light blazing.

What is going on?

I turn around and run for the couch. I land safely on my perch on the top of the couch cushion, but the visibility is terrible. The darkness is growing.

I hear Vacuum approaching. I freeze and sink into the couch. If I don't move, maybe she won't be able to see me. Where is she? She must be right next to the couch by now.

What is she doing?

As soon as I ask the question, I have the answer. Vacuum's arm swoops toward me. I jump in the opposite direction and run for the stairs. I will be safe here. Vacuum can't climb stairs on her own.

The noise fades and stops; I know Vacuum is resting now. I relax and try to figure out what game she is playing with me. She was making the noises to get me downstairs—I am sure of it. But why?

Thump. Thump. Thump.

There she goes again. I ignore the noises this time; I won't give in to her games. The thumps continue several more times.

RRRRROARRRR.

I turn and see Vacuum at the bedroom entrance.

How did she get up the stairs?

Vacuum moves toward me at a lightning-quick speed. Her arm is outstretched and reaching toward my body. I realize this isn't a game anymore. If Vacuum gets any closer, she will suck up all my wrinkles and my curly tail.

Without my wrinkles or curly tail, I won't be a pug!

I jump off the bed and dart past her. I run down the stairs and find a place to hide under the coffee table.

Thump. Thump.

She is coming down the stairs.

Thump. Thump.

The thumps stop. I know she is close. I try to lie still, but I am shaking with fear.

RRRRROARRRR.

I feel the suction of Vacuum's arm on my tail. I'm in trouble. I try to squirm away, but if I run, I might lose my tail. My best chance is to try to rip Vacuum's arm off again. I turn and try to grasp for her, but I don't have enough room to make this move under the table. Instead, I move toward her body. I move out from under the coffee table. I know I only have a split second; I reach for her arm with my jaw. I grab hold and yank it off my tail. The force of my yank frees my tail while I lose control of her arm. The arm flies through the air and lands on my forehead.

Not my wrinkles!

But it's too late. I know it. It doesn't matter if she releases or not. The wrinkles are gone.

My tail might not ever curl again. My life as an adorable pug is over. I close my eyes.

"Mom, why is Zelda twitching and making noises in her sleep?" Lucy asks. I feel a small hand on my forehead.

"Lucy, dogs have dreams just like we do. I bet Zelda was running and barking in her dream," Hannah says.

"Does Zelda have nightmares?" Lucy asks.

"Probably," Hannah says. I open my eyes and look at my fluffy, curly tail. I breathe a sigh of relief. I get up and walk to Vacuum's closet. The door is open; she is sitting at the entrance staring at me.

Thud.

I turn around. Vacuum's arm has fallen next to her, but I am not taking any chances. I run to the couch and sit in Lucy's lap. I look back at Vacuum; she has a devilish smile on her face.

Chapter 7
Zelda and the Pumpkin Bucket

Now that autumn is in full swing, I shiver for the first few minutes of the morning walk. The darkness lasts longer each night, but afternoons provide the perfect walking temperature. I run through leaf piles and chase squirrels as much as I can.

When Ben and Lucy come home from school today, I greet them with my regular round of jumps, licks, and sneezes. I lead them to the back door so we can go outside and play together. But they ignore me and head upstairs.

When they return to the living room, they are wearing the strangest outfits. Lucy has a tail and an extra set of pointy ears. Ben is wearing black that covers his entire body, including his face. All I can see are his eyes.

"When are we leaving, Mom?" Ben asks.

"As soon as your dad gets home," Hannah says. She walks to the kitchen and grabs an orange bucket. She fills it to the brim with treats and sets the bucket on the coffee table. As she sets it down, I realize the bucket has a face with black eyes and nose as well as a toothy smile.

I jump on the couch. I can't see what is in the bucket, and I don't smell anything, either. The treats are probably individually wrapped. I will investigate when the house is empty later. I don't want to put my paws on the coffee table, a punishable offense for a pug.

The door opens, and Nate walks into the living room. He gives Hannah a kiss before giving hugs to Ben and Lucy.

"All right, bunny rabbit and ninja, are we ready to go?" he says.

"Yep, I think so," Hannah responds. They quickly gather a few small orange buckets and head out the door. I watch the car pull out of the driveway from the window. When the coast is clear, I head for the coffee table.

Without hesitation, I jump onto the coffee table. I look into the bucket, but I don't recognize anything. For a second, I think about ignoring the bucket and taking a nap, but I catch a faint whiff of peanut butter. I can't ignore it now; I need to try those treats.

I contemplate trying to get a treat out with my paws, but I probably will knock the whole bucket over. I don't want to clean up a mess. On the other hand, the hole in the bucket looks big enough for my head to fit. It may be a little tight, but it should work.

I carefully stick my head in the bucket and grab a treat with my mouth. I try to back up with the treat in my mouth, but my head is caught. The bucket must have shifted. I move my head over to my right and try again. I get the same result; my head is stuck.

Oh no.

I spit the treat out. I need to get out of the bucket. I can't breathe in this thing. I try to lift my head out, but I hit my head on the handle again. I raise my head and the bucket off the ground. Treats spill onto the coffee table.

Uh oh. Now I've made a mess.

I shake my head and send more treats flying through the air. My head is still stuck.

I stop moving and then try to figure out what to do next. I need to get off this coffee table and onto solid ground. I creep to the edge of the table. If I turn my head down, I can see a little bit of the ground. The jump itself will be easy, but I worry about my bucket head. I go for it anyway.

I jump to the ground and land safely. As I land, the bucket shifts on my head and the treats splatter to the ground, hitting my head on the way. I'm glad I have all the wrinkles and extra skin to cushion me against the impact. I barely feel the treats smacking my head.

But now what?

I blindly walk around the room, unsure where to go. I can't see where I am heading; I only have a glimmer of the floor. I don't know what to do, and it doesn't help that my memory isn't as good as I hoped. I keep running into things—the couch, the chair, and a lamp. I need a plan. If I got my head in the bucket, I have to be able to get it out. I need some leverage, a way to wedge the bucket so I can get my head out.

The lamp!

I walk in the direction of the door and find my way to the pole lamp. I wedge the bucket onto one side of the lamp. I back up, trying to free my head. I feel my head slipping through, so I pull back even harder. But I pull too hard, and the lamp falls toward me. Somehow, I manage to shimmy out of the way as it crashes to the floor in front of the door.

I know I am in deep trouble now. Not only is a bucket on my head with treats covering the coffee table and floor, but I knocked the lamp over and blocked the front door. Maybe I deserve to have this bucket on my head. I wander to the rug in the living room and lie down. I try to fall asleep, but I can't get comfortable. So I lie and wait.

While I wait, I think about all the adventures in the past year. I figured out the leaf piles and made friends with Tucker, Whitney, and Squeaks. I conquered the skate park. I survived the big move to our new home. I even managed to live with Vacuum. But now, I'm going to let an orange bucket get the best of me?

I don't think so.

An idea strikes. I need to get on the couch. I walk over to the couch and back up a few steps. I make the jump with the bucket bouncing on my head. There is no candy left in it now. I miscalculate my jump and smash into the side of the couch. I fall back. I get back up and lift off again. This time, I land on the couch. I creep to the edge of it.

I lean my bucket head over the edge and start shaking. I shake as hard as I can, and the bucket bounces all over my head. I ignore the faint pain and keep shaking. Then I feel it—the sweet feeling of freedom as the bucket flies off my head. It lands on the floor and slides to the other side of the room.

I sit down, panting. My head throbs a bit. The room is a mess. But the bucket is gone. I hear a car door slam. I jump to the floor and grab one of the treats. I tear it open and eat it. It's peanut butter mixed with something even more delicious. I savor the treat, even if it isn't worth the trouble it caused. It's too late to clean up, so I sit down. The door opens a crack until it hits the lamp. Hannah peers inside.

"Why won't this door open?" Hannah says. Ben looks in the front window at the living room.

"Um, Mom, you might want to look at this," he says. Hannah walks to the window.

"Oh my, what a mess! What did Zelda do?" she says. "Let's go in the back door." A minute later, the family walks into the house.

"Zelda, what did you do?" Nate asks as they walk into the disaster zone. I just stare at him with my big, beady pug eyes. "I guess you wanted some candy."

"Looks like she knocked over the lamp," Hannah says.

"How on earth did she do that? Crazy pug." Nate replies.

"Who knows? She is full of secrets," Hannah says. "C'mon, Ben and Lucy, help us clean up the candy before Zelda gets sick from eating it." Ben and Lucy start picking up the treats and putting them back in the smiling orange bucket. After the floor is cleaned up, Lucy walks over and pets my head. It feels so good. Then she whispers in my ear.

"I'll give you candy whenever you want it," Lucy says. She shows me a treat hidden in her hand. "C'mon, follow me." She walks up the stairs to her room. Once we are alone, she hands me the treat. I lick her face, then I dig in.

Chapter 8
Zelda and the Missing Milk–Bone

Now that the leaves are missing from the trees, I have been spending time outside in the yard before the white stuff covers the ground. It is chilly outside, but if the sun is shining I am plenty warm with my pug fur.

"Zelda, do you want a treat?" Nate shouts from the doorway. I run from the back fence to the door.

"Good girl, Zelda," Nate says. I already know what's coming, so I sit and wait patiently.

"Good sit, Zelda. Okay, Zelda. Shake." I quickly raise my right paw to Nate. He shakes it and then bends over and gives me a treat.

It's a Milk-Bone!

I haven't seen one of these in months! At the old house, I used to get a Milk-Bone almost every day in the mail slot. I sat on the couch waiting for the mail lady. When she walked by the window, I knew it was time. She opened the slot and dropped the Milk-Bone along with some pieces of paper and envelope. When I heard the treat drop, I'd run to the closet and find it. Sometimes it landed on the floor; other times the bone was stuck in the slot. I'd use my paws to knock it out. Most days, I didn't eat the Milk-Bone right away. Instead, I would find a place to hide it, like in my dog bed or under a blanket. When I was hungry the next day, I would retrieve the bone and enjoy its crunchy goodness.

One day, the mail lady turned into a mailman and the Milk-Bones stopped appearing in the mail slot. I was depressed about it for weeks, but eventually I forgot all about the mail lady and the mail slot. Until now.

Once again, I have a Milk-Bone. I grab it with my mouth and walk away. I look around the living room, searching for the perfect spot to hide it. I need to keep it safe until I need a late-night snack.

With Hannah and Lucy in the living room, I decide it is a better idea to hide the bone upstairs. I walk upstairs into Lucy's room. Her bed is a mess with blankets and pillows everywhere.

Perfect.

I jump onto the bed and dig for the best hiding spot. With the blankets out of the way, I lay the Milk-Bone on the bed. I drag the blankets over it. I take a step back. I can smell the bone, but I can't see it. That will do.

I jump off the bed and run downstairs. I find a toy and play tug-of-war with Lucy. A few minutes later, I grow tired and cuddle up on the couch next to Hannah. I fall asleep.

When I wake up, I am starving. I take a walk to the food bowl and have a few bites when I remember the Milk-Bone. I run upstairs to Lucy's room. The lights are out; she is already asleep. I jump on the bed, careful not to wake her. I nuzzle my way under the covers toward the bottom of the bed where I left the Milk-Bone. I begin to suspect it is missing when I smell nothing. Sure enough, it's gone. Disappointed and frustrated, I decide to go to bed. I curl up with Lucy and fall asleep.

The next day I wake up recharged and refreshed. It's not the first time I've lost a toy or bone. I'm sure I will get another one. I will have to find a better hiding spot for it.

My day passes like many others. I go for a walk in the neighborhood and a romp in the backyard with Lucy and Ben. When I come inside, Lucy walks to the treat cabinet.

"Do you want a treat, Zelda?" she asks. I wait patiently as she pulls a Milk-Bone out of a box and hands it to me.

"Here you go," she says. I grab it and run to the living room. Today, the living room is empty and perfect for milk-bone hiding. I bury it in the blanket on the couch. When I finish burying it, Lucy is staring at me. I ignore her stares and find a blue Nylabone to chew.

The evening passes by like most other days. I go for a walk with Ben and play with Nate. They eat dinner at the table while Ben passes little bits under the table to me. When Lucy disappears upstairs, I know it's time for bed. But first I want to check on my Milk-Bone. I hop onto the couch and move the blanket aside.

The Milk-Bone is gone again!

This time I investigate further. I check in the crevices of the couch and under the pillows. I find nothing. Dejected, I wander upstairs to bed and fall asleep with Lucy.

The next day, I am determined to find the culprit behind the Milk-Bone disappearances. I wait patiently all day until Hannah gives me one in the afternoon. I hide it in the blanket on the couch and find a perfect lookout spot across the room on the chair. I lie down and wait.

When I wake up, Lucy and Ben are home from school. I really want to greet them with a lick and maybe a sneeze, but I stay put. I don't want to take my eyes off the Milk-Bone.

"Hey Mom, is Zelda feeling okay?" Ben asks. He walks over and pets my head.

"I think so, why?" Hannah responds.

"She didn't greet us when we walked in. She just stayed on the chair," Ben says.

"That is a little strange," she says. "Let's keep our eye on her today." Lucy walks over and sits next to me.

"I'm sorry you aren't feeling good," she whispers. My plan is already being foiled. They think I am sick and won't take their eyes off me. How am I supposed to find the Milk-Bone thief? Lucy and Ben wander away from me into the kitchen.

"Can I give Zelda a treat to make her feel better?" Lucy asks. I perk up.

"No, honey, that might make her feel worse. Let's wait and see. If she seems fine later, you can give her a treat," Hannah says.

Oh geez. Now I've lost an opportunity for a treat.

I maintain my lookout on the chair, trying to come up with a new plan. As I brainstorm, Lucy returns from the kitchen and sits on the couch, right on top of the Milk-Bone hiding spot.

"What is this?" she asks. She digs through the blanket and recovers the Milk-Bone.

"A Milk-Bone! Zelda, do you want it?" I remain motionless, not sure what to do.

"How about I put it in your bed for safekeeping?" Lucy says. I nod. The bed is across from the couch, still in view from my spot. I watch Lucy walk to my dog bed. Instead of placing it on top of the bed, she hides it under the pillow.

"There you go, Z Bug. It's safe with the others," she says.

Wait a minute. With the others?

I break my stakeout and dash to the dog bed. I rip the cushion off the bed and toss it across the room. Staring at me are three delicious, untouched Milk-Bones. I turn and look at a smiling Lucy, the Milk-Bone thief. I should have known. Lucy is the other mischievous one in the house. I grab one and gobble it up. When I finish eating, the room is empty. Lucy is in the kitchen. I grab the cushion and drag it over top of the two remaining Milk-Bones. Lucy will think I moved the bones or ate them. They are safe here. At least I hope they are safe.

Chapter 9
Zelda and Norman

When Nate mentions the word *ride*, I know it will be a good day. I run in eleven circles around him until he grabs me and harnesses me. All five of us load up in his black car and drive away. I bounce around in the back seat from Lucy's lap to Ben's lap. Once we get out of the neighborhood, I don't recognize the busy, fast street; we must be going somewhere new. Watching the cars speed by makes me dizzy, so I find a comfortable spot in Ben's lap and lie down. When the car slows down, I pop up and look outside. We are driving in a neighborhood filled with houses. Eventually, we pull into a driveway and stop.

I jump from one side of the car to the other, from the front to back, waiting for someone to open a door. They are so slow. I'm ready to go! Finally Nate grabs me, leashes me, and lets me out of the car. I dash for the grass; the smell overwhelms me.

A dog lives here!

And then I hear it—the deep bark of a dog. I halt my lawn exploration and pull Nate toward the door.

"Zelda, wait!" Nate shouts. We stop, and Hannah opens the front door and heads inside. I lunge for the door again. I don't want Hannah to go in the house alone. But I can't move anywhere with Nate holding my leash. The barking stops. I hope Hannah is okay.

When the door opens, it's a familiar face, but not Hannah. Next to her is the source of the deep bark. He is brown with some white around his nose, chest, and front paws. He is maybe seven pugs' worth with a giant wrinkly face.

He has more wrinkles than I do!

I sit in awe. I'm pretty sure his head is the size of my entire body.

"Okay Zelda, do you want to meet Norman?" asks Nate. We walk slowly to the dog. I bark a few times to let him know I'm coming. He whimpers back. I approach him and take a sniff, waiting for a response. He returns the sniff and then looks at me with his big droopy face. I can tell from his eyes and calm demeanor that he is friendly.

"Good dogs," I hear someone say.

I wonder if he will play with me?

I run toward him and nip at his wrinkles. He follows suit and chases me until we are both yanked back by our leashes.

"I think they are fine. Want to let them loose in the backyard?" Hannah asks.

"Sure," the familiar woman says. I've seen her at our house a few times before.

We are led around the side of the house and through a gate. As soon as we are unleashed, I start running. Norman chases after me and catches me quickly. He is fast! We roll around in the yard. He is surprisingly gentle with his giant mouth. We play all afternoon while everybody else stays inside. I don't even mind that they left us outside in the cold because we have each other.

"It's time to go home," Nate says. Norman and I are lying in the grass panting and resting. "C'mon, Zelda, time for a ride. Let's go home," Nate says again. As I get up, I realize I am exhausted. Norman wore me out, but it was worth it.

For the next few days, I eagerly listen for the words *ride* or *Norman*. I can't wait to visit his house again. I already know he is my best friend. Tucker and Whitney would rather play with each other than me. Jack Jack spends his time hiding from me or hissing at me. Since the move, I haven't seen Squeaks, and Nate won't let me meet the dog behind our backyard fence. But the days pass without mention of Norman or any car trips. I start to lose hope that I will ever see Norman again.

"What time are your sister and everyone coming over?" Nate asks. I perk my ears up. Ben and Lucy are upstairs. Hannah, Nate, and I are in the kitchen.

"She should be here around seven," she says.

"Is she bringing Norman, too?" he asks.

"Yep."

"This should be fun," Nate says.

Norman is coming over!

I pug sprint throughout the house—to the living room, up the stairs into Lucy's room, then down the stairs into the living room. When I reach the kitchen, I stop for some water.

"I think Zelda is excited," Hannah says.

"Yes, she is. But she'd better save some energy for when Norman comes over," Nate replies. He is right. Norman is much bigger than I. I need my rest to keep up. I walk to the couch and lie down. But my excitement level is too high, and I can't sleep. I find a bone and channel my energy into chewing.

A few minutes later, I hear car doors slam and then voices. I jump on the top of the couch and look out the window.

There he is!

I wait eagerly by the door. When they open the door and let him loose, we go running. We run through the living room and kitchen. Norman slides all over the place, slamming into the kitchen table along the way. I run up the stairs, and Norman chases me.

"Zelda, want to go outside?" I hear Nate yell. I dart down the stairs for the back door. Nate opens the door, and Norman and I both go running. We sprint in circles around the yard. I use my maneuverability to my advantage, making quick turns to keep Norman off my heels. Eventually I slow a bit, and he rams into me. We tumble and play. I bite his huge lips and ears while he licks my face. We lie together for a few minutes before I realize how thirsty I am. I walk to the door to get a drink inside. I take long drinks of water. Norman waits for me to finish and then drinks the rest of the bowl in two big gulps.

I need a rest from the chase game, so I wander into the living room with my family and the guests. I lie next to Norman, panting and smiling. A few minutes later, Norman and his family leave. I wish Norman could stay with us, but I understand he has his own family and home. But it sure would be nice to have a friend around every day.

Chapter 10
A Pug Thanksgiving

When Hannah told me we were going to see Tucker and Whitney, I was super excited. I couldn't wait to play with them and chase Jack Jack, the cat. Now that I have arrived, my excitement is waning. The house is filled to the brim with people of all sizes—from tiny children to giant men. Anywhere I go, someone wants to pet my head or pick me up. Ben and Lucy are running around with other children; Hannah and Nate are ignoring me. I can't escape the madness.

With all the commotion in the house, I follow the lead of Tucker and Whitney. I curl up on the couch next to Whitney, who is between two unfamiliar bodies. I try to fall asleep, but the noise in the house is deafening. It's no use. I get up and wander toward the kitchen, following my nose. The smell is overwhelming but in the best possible way. I wonder what they are cooking.

The kitchen is busy with activity; I have to walk carefully to avoid being trampled. My nose leads me in front of the oven. Unfortunately, the oven is in the center of the kitchen, surrounded by moving feet. I take a step back and try to see in the oven, but I am too short to look in the window.

I see a foot coming toward me, and I jump to the right. I can't stay in the kitchen any longer if I want to stay in one piece. I walk back to the couch and jump up next to Tucker. From this spot, I have the perfect vantage point of the kitchen. I sit and wait, hoping to see what is giving off the delicious odor.

Not long after I sit down, the kitchen mysteriously clears. Most of the group vacates to the living room. I leave my spot on the couch, and someone claims my seat moments later. I don't mind. I'm willing to give it up to figure out what is cooking in the kitchen.

I walk straight to the oven and stand on my hind legs. The oven is warm to the touch on my paws. I look into the window. The window is dark, but I can make out the outline of something. It is big and sort of round with a pale color. I have never seen anything like it. Honestly, it looks disgusting. I jump back from the oven, disappointed.

How could something so ugly smell so good?

I wander around the kitchen looking for scraps. I find a few bits of cheese and crackers under the table before returning to the living room. A spot is open next to Hannah, so I claim it and lie down.

I can't sleep with the noise and activity. After what seems like an eternity of trying to fall asleep, I watch Hannah carefully get off the couch and head to the kitchen. I follow her.

"Is the bird ready to take out?" she asks.

Bird? That's one big bird.

"I think so."

"Great! That means it's almost dinnertime," she says. "Z, come here." She walks away from the oven to the other side of the kitchen.

We watch as Nate's dad opens the oven door and reaches inside. He pulls out something completely different from what I saw. It is golden brown, almost a pug-color brown. It looks moist and tender. And, oh my, the smell. It reminds me of chicken but yummier. I need to get a piece.

"The turkey looks and smells great," Hannah says as Nate's dad places it on the table.

Turkey? What kind of bird is a turkey?

I hop onto a chair in the kitchen and stare at the magnificent cooked turkey bird. While I fixate on it, the rest of the kitchen is a blur. People are moving everywhere and carrying food to the table, to the counter, and back again. They are shouting to one another and laughing, so I sit and wait. The turkey bird is unreachable at the moment, but at some point I know an opportunity will arise for me to take a sample bite. Or two. Or three.

I watch as Nate's dad cuts up the turkey bird. I am a little sad watching the giant bird dismantled into bite-sized pieces. But in the long run, I know it's better for me if it is sliced. It's a lot easier for me to get my paws on a slice than on the whole big turkey bird.

All the food, including slices of the bird, is resting on the counter in the middle of the kitchen. It's impossible for me to reach the counter unless someone lifts me up. Eventually the food will move to plates around the table, and the opportunity will come.

The seats are filling up around me. Children and adults are staking their claims on chairs. I know it's only a matter of time before someone sits on me, so I hop to the ground. I look for the kids' section of the table, the gold mine for scavenging.

Lucy sits down on the far end of the long table. The table is the longest I have ever seen. You could have twenty pugs sitting on chairs! Sitting next to Lucy is a small boy. He is the lucky winner today; he will be my helper on the turkey quest.

In a few minutes, the room is quiet and the table is full with people and plates. I sit next to the small boy and wait. He eats for a few minutes and then stops. He backs his chair up.

"Christopher, you need to eat more before you get up," a woman says from across the room.

"But Mom, I'm not hungry," the boy says.

"You need to eat the rest of your turkey and potatoes." The boy looks at his plate. I take my opportunity. I walk over to his far side, hidden from his mom's view. I put my front paws on his lap.

"Hi, Zelda," he whispers.

This is it. I know it.

I leap onto his lap. My head is at table height, but I can't reach the turkey. I put a paw on the table.

"Zelda, down," Hannah yells from the far end of the table.

It's now or never.

I put my other paw on the plate and reach for the slice of turkey. I grab for it with my mouth, but as I put my weight on my front paws, the plate flips toward me. The turkey flies to me, and I catch it in my mouth. I leap off the table and onto the ground and out of the way. With the turkey in my mouth, I look up.

Uh oh.

The plate is upside down on the boy's lap.

I'm in trouble.

I bolt for the living room, but I slow down when I hear laughter. I stop and turn, setting the turkey on the floor. The table is erupting with laughter; I am okay. I listen to the conversation as I take my first bite.

"I can't believe what just happened."

"Zelda must have really wanted some turkey."

"Christopher, let's get you cleaned up."

"This will be something to remember for years."

I savor the turkey. It does remind me of chicken, but juicier. After the first bite, I gobble the rest in seconds.

"Happy Thanksgiving, Zelda," Nate shouts. The table laughs. I lick my lips and smile.

Chapter 11
Zelda and the Stuffed Animal

The next weeks pass by quietly. Winter has arrived in dramatic fashion with frigid temperatures and cold winds. The pine tree has appeared in our living room again. I spend most of my days under a blanket, lacking the ambition to move, let alone hide toys from the pine tree or find a new adventure. I haven't seen Norman for a few weeks; I wish he would come for a visit.

My family is out for the day, so I await their return in my dog bed. Occasionally a warm breeze blows from the wall behind me. I dream of warm weather, chasing Norman, and hiding Milk-Bones. When I awake, the family is walking through the door carrying a few shopping bags. Lucy carries her bag upstairs.

"I think that was a successful Christmas shopping trip. We got most of the family done," Hannah says.

"Yes, including Lucy," Ben says.

"I couldn't say no to her. She loved the dog; it looks just like Zelda," Hannah says.

"You said no to my request for a new video game," Ben whines.

"Sorry, dear, Christmas is coming, I'm sure Santa will bring you something you want," Nate says.

"Yeah, yeah," Ben says, sitting down on the couch. Maybe I can cheer him up. I jump up on the seat next to him and give him a big kiss. He smiles and mumbles, "I love you, too, Zelda."

That evening, I follow Ben upstairs to bed. He turns into his room, but I head across the hall to my sleeping spot next to Lucy. I jump on the bed. Lucy stirs, which lets me under the covers. I fall asleep instantly.

When I wake up, light is streaming into the room. Lucy is already up and out of bed. A small fawn pug is staring at me from across the room on top of a shelf. I blink a few times to make sure I am awake and seeing the world right. The pug is still there, looking directly at me from its perch. Is it stuck on the shelf? Maybe it needs help. I start barking.

There is no response from the pug. Strange. It's also odd that I don't smell the dog, either. How is it camouflaging its odor? I have so many questions. I look around the room to find a path up to the shelf. But there is no way up there. Even with my great pug leaping ability, I can't make the jump from the bed to the shelf.

How did it get there?

I need to get help so it can get down and we can be friends. I walk out of the room. I hear my family talking downstairs.

"When do we pick up Peach?" I hear as I walk down the stairs.

"In a week or two, whenever the rescue says she is ready," Nate says. I have no clue what they are talking about. Don't they know a pug is trapped upstairs? I start barking.

"Hi, Zelda," Lucy says. I bark some more, but the family mostly ignores me. I don't even know why I try barking anymore; they never understand what I'm trying to communicate. It's time for Plan B.

I grab a toy and bring it to Ben. When he reaches for it, I jump backward so he can't grab it. I do this a few more times to get him excited and playing. Then, I race upstairs hoping Ben or someone else will follow. I stop at the top of the stairs and listen for movement. Nothing.

"Zelda, c'mon, let's play downstairs," Ben yells. The plan failed. I walk back into Lucy's room and check on the pug. It is still sitting on the shelf. I wander back downstairs. Eventually someone will come upstairs. When they do, I'll make sure they see the pug.

After an hour of waiting, Hannah walks upstairs. I walk straight to Lucy's bedroom and start barking. After a few minutes, Hannah joins me in Lucy's room.

"Why are you barking?" she asks. I look at the motionless pug. "Oh Zelda, that's just a stuffed animal. Leave it be," she says and walks away. I sit dumbfounded. I have no idea what she is talking about.

Stuffed animal?

I jump on Lucy's bed and wait for the next person to wander up the stairs. Only a few minutes pass before Lucy appears in the doorway.

"Hi, Zelda Bug," she says. "What are you doing?" I look at her and then at the pug. I bark a few times.

"What is it?" she says, petting my forehead. It feels so good. I start fading into pug dreamland.

Wait a minute. I need to focus.

I start barking and stealing quick glances at the pug on the shelf. But Lucy keeps petting me, ignoring the other pug. It's so hard to concentrate when she massages my head.

When I wake up, I am alone on the bed. I look up at the shelf.

The pug is gone!

I spring out of bed and search the room. No sign of the pug. I move through the rest of the bedrooms upstairs, but I see no trace of it. I continue my search on the bottom level. Lucy is sitting on the couch with the pug in her lap.

The pug is okay.

I breathe a sigh of relief and run downstairs. I jump on the couch next to the pug. I start barking, but the pug does nothing. Plus, I still can't smell the pug. I can't even tell if it's a girl or a boy. I walk over Lucy's lap and playfully nip at the pug. Nothing. I try one more time, this time grabbing hold of its leg. The leg is soft, like one of my toys. I grab hold and yank, but I lose my grip. The pug goes flying across the room. As it sails through the air, I realize my mistake. The pug isn't real: it's a toy, just like my owl. I was so excited to have another pug in the house that I missed all the signs. The pug didn't move, bark, sneeze, or snore. I couldn't even smell it. I pick up the pug I flung across the room and bring it to Lucy. Of course, the pug was a toy; I just wanted it to be real.

Chapter 12
Zelda Meets Peach

After the incident with the fake pug, I am staying low key around the house. Honestly, I am a little embarrassed at my mistake. My family, on the other hand, is busy with activity. Hannah is covering boxes during the day and placing them under the tree. I notice Hannah and Nate talking in hushed voices about "presents." Lucy is running around the house mumbling about "Santa Claus." Even Ben is more talkative and playful than normal. He keeps telling me how much I am going to love my Christmas present.

I watch and listen from my perch on top of the couch. I can tell we are getting close to the big day, the day when everyone unwraps all the presents under the pine tree.

"Okay, Zelda, we will be back later," Ben says. "Tomorrow is the big day." The family leaves without me. I watch the white stuff fall on the grass from the window. I hope I will get a new owl. Or Milk-Bones. Or a Nylabone. Or all of them. Christmas is the best.

When my family returns home, the snow is illuminating the darkness outside. My family greets me. Hannah and Nate send Ben and Lucy to bed. I am warm and toasty in my blanket, so I stay downstairs with Hannah and Nate. After a few minutes of conversation, Nate gets up and leaves the house.

"Zelda, it's bedtime," Hannah says. We walk upstairs together. I jump onto Lucy's bed while Hannah checks on Ben. When Hannah returns, she gives Lucy a kiss and pets me. She says goodnight to us and closes the door.

I wake up in the middle of the night to a scratching noise. I want to bark, but everyone is sleeping. I don't want to get in trouble. I listen for a few more minutes to the scratching. I hear a few whispers and the scratching stops. I fall back asleep.

The next time I wake up, Lucy is moving out of bed. It must be early; only a few streams of light are peaking through the window. As we walk down the stairs, Lucy is mumbling about Christmas and Santa.

Hannah and Nate are waiting downstairs. The pine tree is lit, and the number of gifts under the tree has doubled.

"Merry Christmas," Nate shouts to Lucy and me.

"Shhhh," Hannah says. "You will wake up Ben."

"It's time for him to get up anyway. It's Christmas morning—time for gifts!" he replies. Lucy wanders down the stairs and sits in front of the tree.

"Wow, look at all these presents Santa brought," she says. I hear a few creaks from above, and a few minutes later, Ben appears on the stairs.

"Merry Christmas," Nate shouts again.

"Merry Christmas," Ben replies. He walks down the stairs and takes a seat on the couch.

The fun begins. Presents are passed around, and the family opens the gifts. I run around and investigate all the new toys and objects. So far, there isn't much for me. Only a few gifts remain when I hear a whimper from upstairs. And then, the scratching noise returns.

What is upstairs?

I run up the stairs. The whimpering and scratching is originating from Hannah and Nate's room, but the door is closed. Hannah and Nate appear next to me.

"You grab Zelda," Nate says, "And I will get Peach." Hannah bends over and picks me up. Nate opens the door, and a dog runs out.

What?

I squirm and break loose from Hannah's arms and chase the dog down the stairs. When I arrive downstairs, the dog is licking Ben's face. She is dark brown and white with tall ears. She is bigger than me, but not by much. She doesn't have a long snout, but she also doesn't have wrinkles.

"Merry Christmas, Lucy and Zelda—meet Peach, the Boston terrier, our new dog," Nate says. Peach wanders over to Lucy and starts licking her face. I stand motionless, unsure what to do.

Did I hear Nate correctly? Is Peach here to stay?

I walk up to Peach and bark a few times. She doesn't seem to mind. When I get close, she backs away from Lucy. I nip at her front leg, and she allows it. She reciprocates, and we start rolling on the floor together. I find my owl and she chases me, trying to get it from me. When she finally grabs hold, we play tug-of-war.

"Well, I think they will get along fine," Hannah says.

"Lucy, do you like Peach?" Nate asks.

"Yes, she's nice. And now Zelda has a friend." Lucy says.

"Yes, she does," Nate replies.

"She's so friendly and sweet," Ben says.

"We definitely got lucky with Peach," Hannah replies. "And with Zelda. She's turned out to be a pretty good dog."

"Yes, she is," Ben says. I take a break from tug-of-war and wander over to Hannah, who is sitting on the couch again. I jump in her lap and give her a kiss. Peach follows my lead, and we both are in Hannah's lap and giving her kisses. I have a friend to play with all the time. Even better, I have a family who loves me enough to find me a friend. My pug life is awesome. It's another merry Christmas!

A Sneak Peek into
The Adventures of Zelda:
Pug and Peach

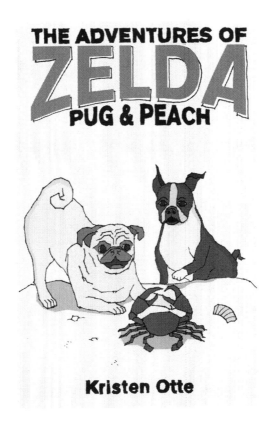

Available Now

Chapter 1
The Mouth Game

I jump on Lucy's bed and curl up under the covers with her for the night. I close my eyes and let the exhaustion take over. My pug body is tired after a long day of playing and chasing my brand new sister. My sister is my Christmas gift. She was the best gift ever—making me the happiest pug on the planet. She is a Boston terrier, and her name is Peach.

Peach is a little bigger than I am, with tall, pointy ears, droopy lips, and a pug-like smashed face. Peach doesn't have nearly the number of wrinkles I do. She is dark, brindled-brown with patches of white, including a white stripe down her head to her nose, and a small peach spot on her nose. I think that's why she is named Peach. Although she is a good-looking dog, Peach is not as pretty as me, especially since she doesn't have a curly tail. Her tail is short and a bit crooked. Honestly, I don't really care what she looks like; I am just excited to have a canine friend.

When I open my eyes the next day, light shines through the window, and the spot next to me is empty. Lucy is awake already. I stand and stretch—my body isn't used to all this exercise during the cold season. I hear movement downstairs as I go through my morning round of sneezes.

My family is gathered in the living room and eating breakfast. I see Peach nestled in a spot between Lucy and Hannah on the couch. Lucy is laughing as Peach repeatedly licks Lucy's face. I feel a pang of envy rip through me, but I ignore it and walk into the kitchen.

I smell bacon!

Nate is cooking in the kitchen, so I sit patiently next to him. If I stay calm, I am sure he will give me a piece of bacon. But it is so hard to remain calm when bacon is at stake. I sit and stare. I can't see the bacon, but the smell is overpowering.

Ruff. Ruff.

"Zelda, quiet," Nate says. I sit again. I didn't mean to bark, but I couldn't help it. Peach wanders into the kitchen.

"Hi, Peach," Nate says. "Do you want some bacon?" Peach trots over to Nate and starts leaping into the air.

She is springy!

"I think that means yes," Nate says, laughing. I inch closer to him. He better not forget about me. Nate grabs a piece of bacon. I do my best sit and stare at Nate with my bulgy, brown eyes.

"Good sit, Zelda," he says. "Peach, can you sit?" Peach continues to leap for the bacon while I wait patiently like the model pug that I am.

"No, Peach," he says and tries to get Peach to sit.

How long will I have to wait?

Finally, Peach sits, and Nate gives her a piece of the bacon.

"Good girl, Zelda," he says and gives me the remaining bacon. I scarf it up in a second.

"Okay, that's it for now. You're free," he says. I walk to the living room. Peach follows.

I find a comfortable spot on the couch next to Lucy. Peach jumps onto the couch and squeezes into the spot next to me. I look at her, and she nips at my face in a playful manner. I bite back, aiming for her mouth, but she shifts out of the way. I try again; this time she opens her mouth as mine approaches. We lock mouths, attempting to maneuver our mouths over top each other's.

We shift and squirm as the game continues, trying to get an advantage. Peach ends up upside down on Ben's lap. I jump on top of Peach, confident that I have her mouth cornered.

"Mom, what's happening?" Ben asks. I snap at Peach, but she dodges to the right. I pause for a moment to listen.

"They are playing, don't worry about it," Hannah says.

Oh, good. Hannah understands.

While I am distracted, Peach nips for my neck. I jerk backward just in time.

"They seem like they are trying to hurt each other," Ben says.

"No, this is how dogs play. If they were trying to hurt each other, you would know," Hannah says. "Although this is a funny game they are playing." I go in for the final bite.

I have her mouth!

"It kind of seems like they are trying to figure out whose mouth is bigger," Ben says. Hannah laughs.

"It does," Hannah responds.

I have Peach's mouth for only seconds before she wiggles her way out of the hold. But the moment of victory supercharges me. I leap off the couch and sprint around the coffee table, into the dining room, sliding as I go, and back to the living room. I jump to the couch and give Peach a quick nip, urging her to follow my next move. I leap again, but this time I run up the stairs and away from the slippery floor. I hear thumps behind me, and I know Peach is following. She catches up to me quickly, and I run under Lucy's bed. She's unable to fit, so she stops and barks at me. I lie on the floor panting for a few minutes. Peach keeps barking.

"What's going on up here?" Nate asks. He walks into the room. Peach stands on her hind legs and licks his hand. I crawl out from the bed.

"Oh, hi, Zelda. Come on, let's go downstairs," he says. We follow him downstairs to the living room. I see an open blanket.

"It looks like they are done playing the 'Whose Mouth Is Bigger' game," Ben says.

For now, but we will play again.

AFTERWORD

Thank you for purchasing this book. Zelda's adventures continue in *The Adventures of Zelda: Pug and Peach.*

If you enjoyed this book, please leave a review at Amazon or Goodreads. In addition, I invite you to visit my website and join my email list to receive updates on my latest writing projects.

In addition, I want to thank a few people who were big supporters of this project. First, thanks to my family for supporting my writing career and everything I do. A special thanks to my mother who constantly reminds me of the proper place to put commas and proofreads my work. Thank you to my editor, Candace Johnson, for her hard work and kind words. Thanks to Michael McFarland for designing another awesome cover. Thanks to my husband, Brian, for not thinking I am crazy for pursuing a career in writing and supporting me every step of the way. And finally, thanks to our pug, Zelda, for inspiring these stories and bringing joy and laughter into our home.

ABOUT THE AUTHOR

Author Kristen Otte writes books for children, teens, and adults. Her mission is to bring joy and laughter through stories to people young and old. When she isn't writing or reading, you may find her on the basketball court coaching her high school girls' team. If she isn't writing or coaching, she is probably chasing her husband and dogs around the house.

BOOKS BY KRISTEN OTTE

The Adventures of Zelda: A Pug Tale
The Adventures of Zelda: The Second Saga
The Adventures of Zelda: Pug and Peach
The Adventures of Zelda: The Four Seasons
The Photograph
The Evolution of Lillie Gable

Learn more about Kristen, her books, and her workshops at her website:
www.kristenotte.com.

Made in the USA
Middletown, DE
17 August 2017